Let's Find Mimi
On Holiday

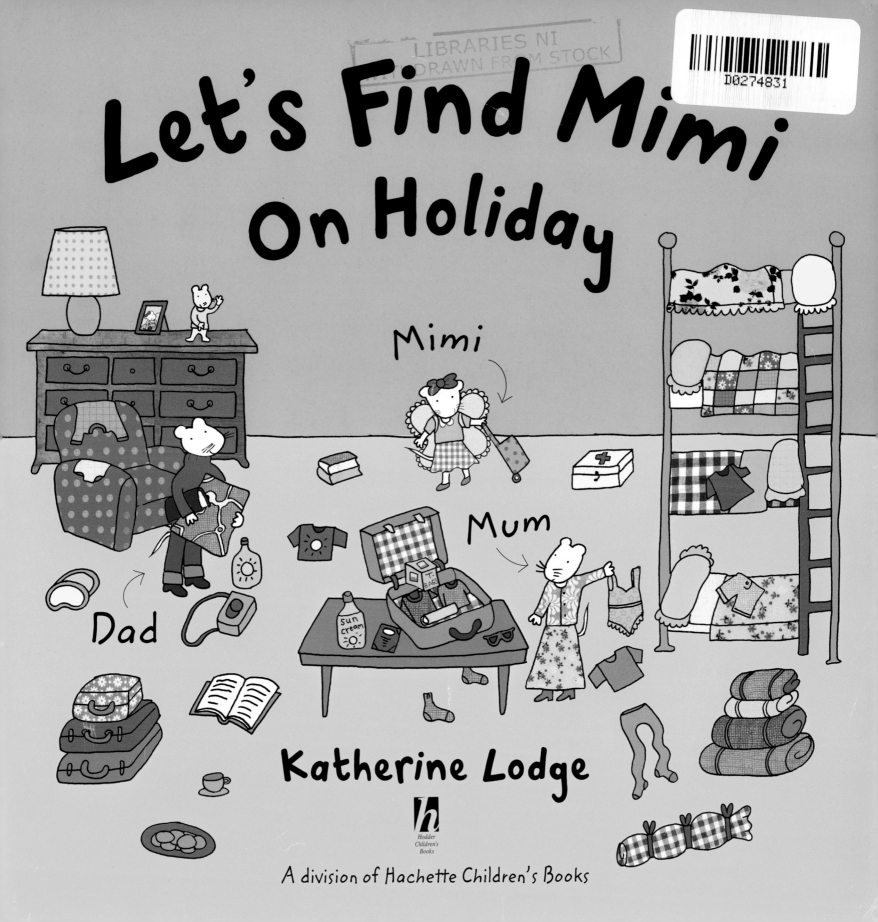

Mimi

Mum

Dad

Katherine Lodge

Hodder Children's Books

A division of Hachette Children's Books

It's time for Mimi's holiday.
She's at the airport on her way!

Can you see **Mimi** wheeling a **spotty suitcase?**

CHECK-IN

Security

X-RAY

PASSPORTS

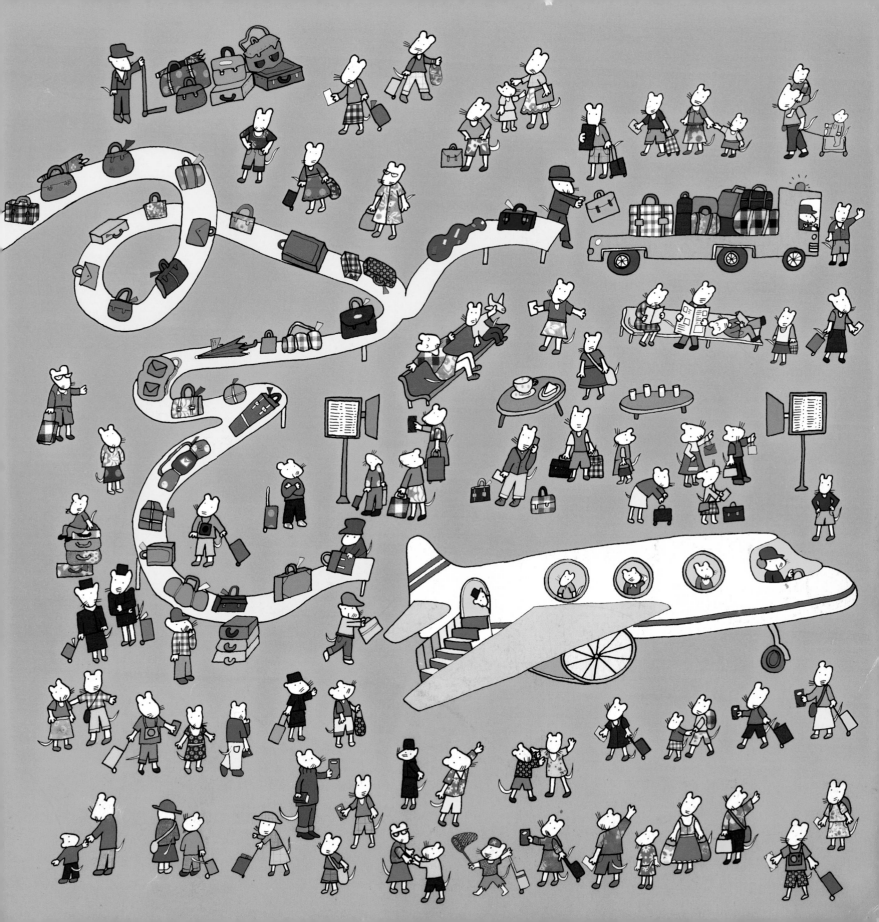

The campervan is packed — let's go!
Where's Mimi heading, do you know?

Can you see **Mimi** and **Mum**

climbing into a **campervan?**

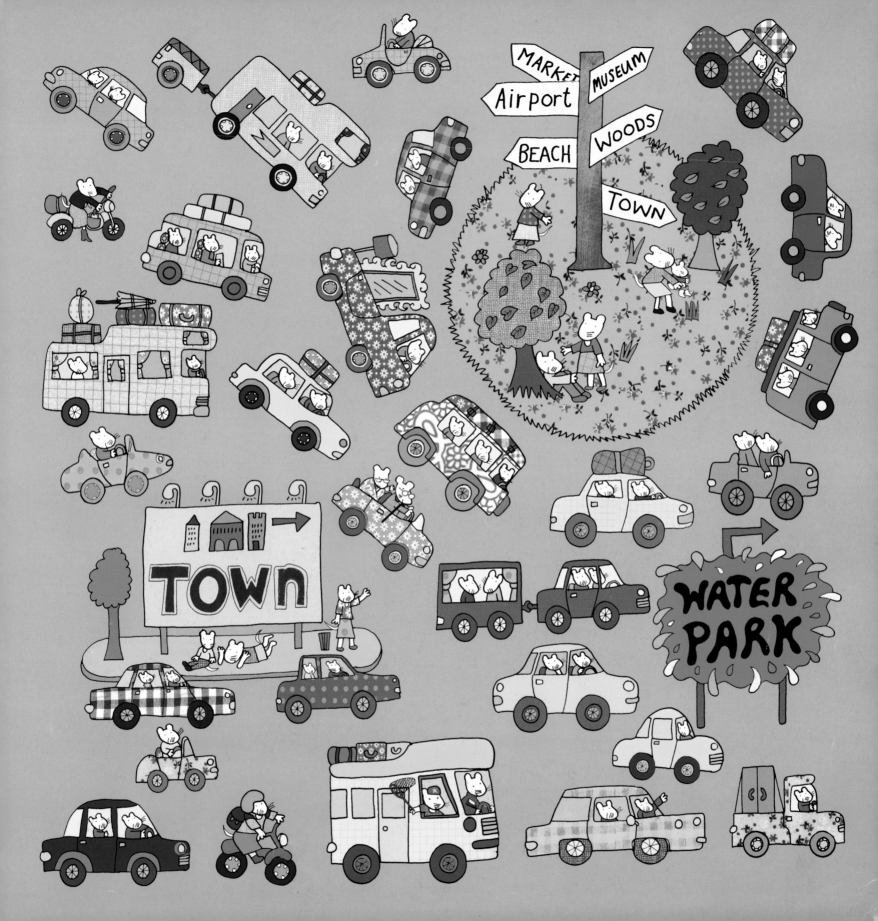

MARKET
MUSEUM
Airport
WOODS
BEACH
TOWN

TOWN

WATER PARK

Now Mimi's having lots of fun
Playing beach games in the sun.

Can you see Mimi and Aunty Mel
playing with a bat and ball?

Sailing on the clear blue sea
Is Mimi's favourite place to be!

Can you see **Mimi** and **Grandpa fishing?**

The Royal Cheese

WHISKERS

Whoosh! Whee! Splash! Watch Mimi ride
On the waterpark's big slide.
Can you see Mimi on the slide?

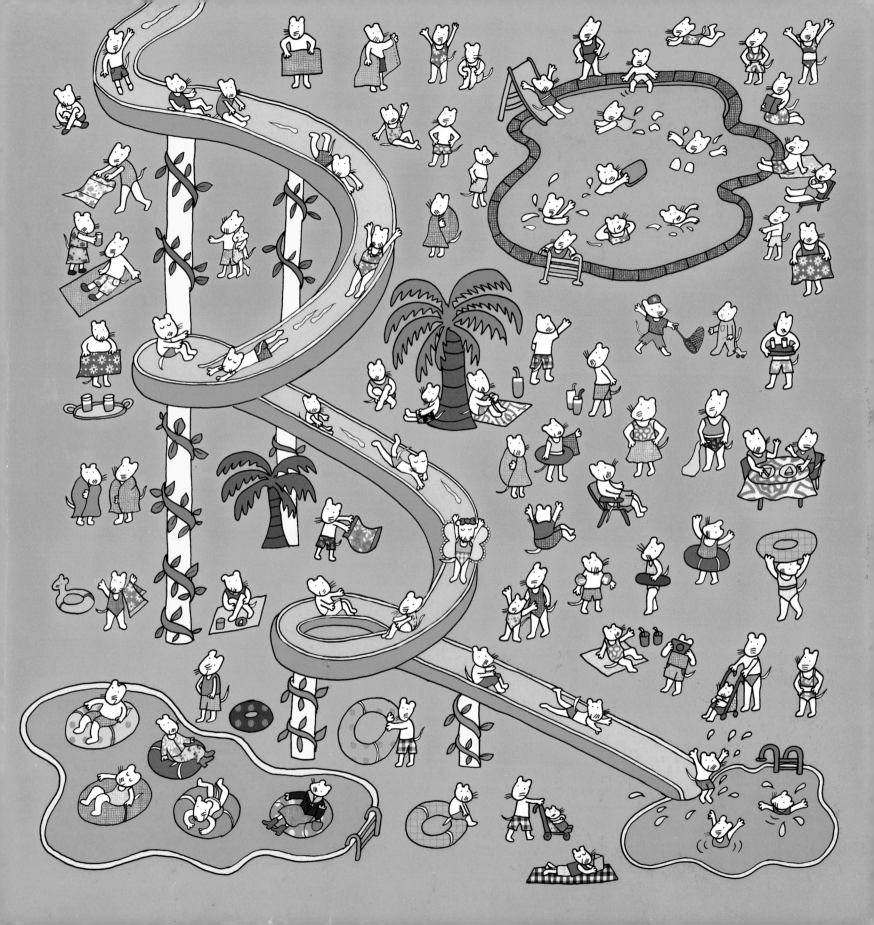

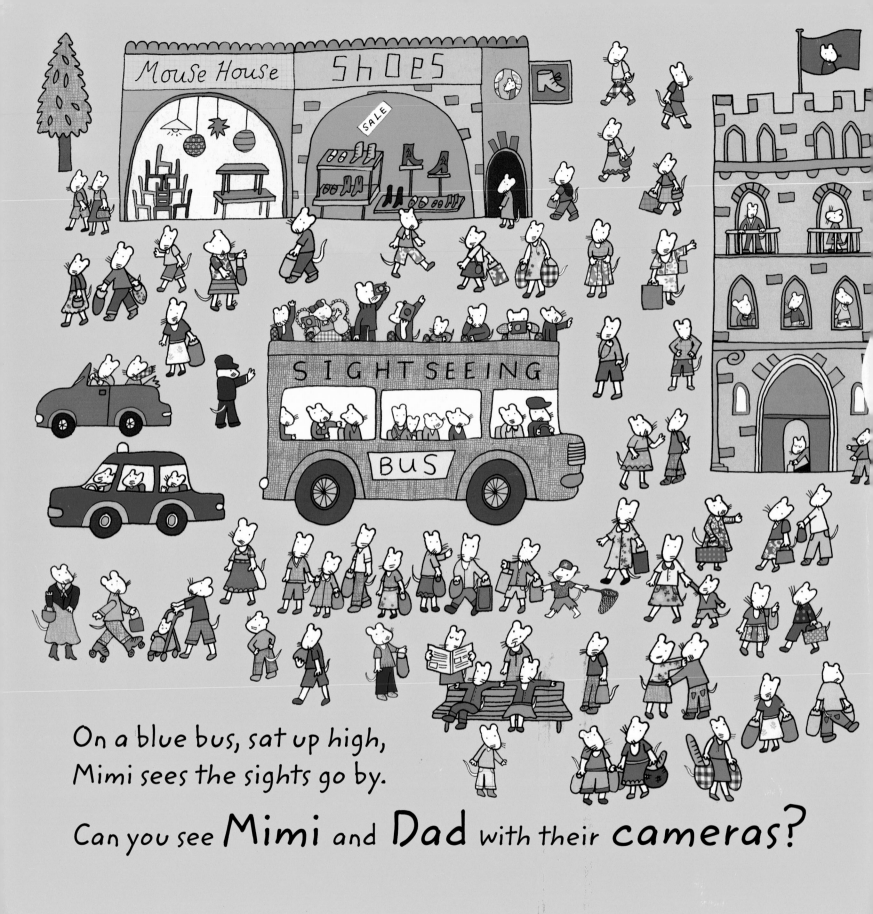

On a blue bus, sat up high,
Mimi sees the sights go by.

Can you see **Mimi** and **Dad** with their **cameras?**

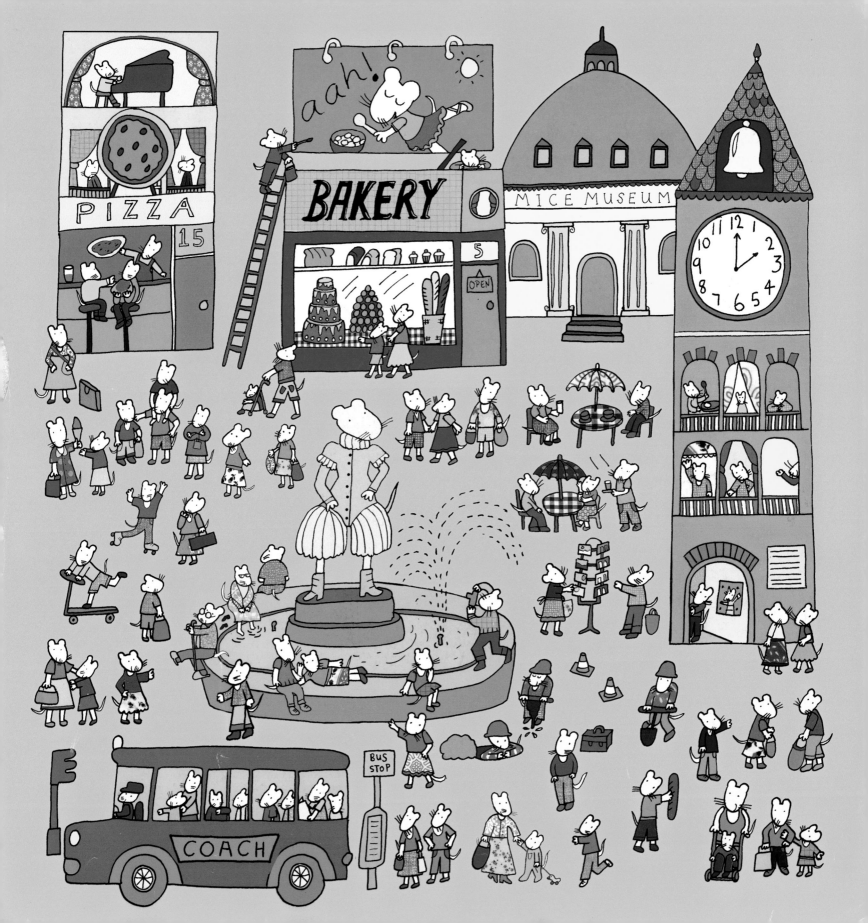

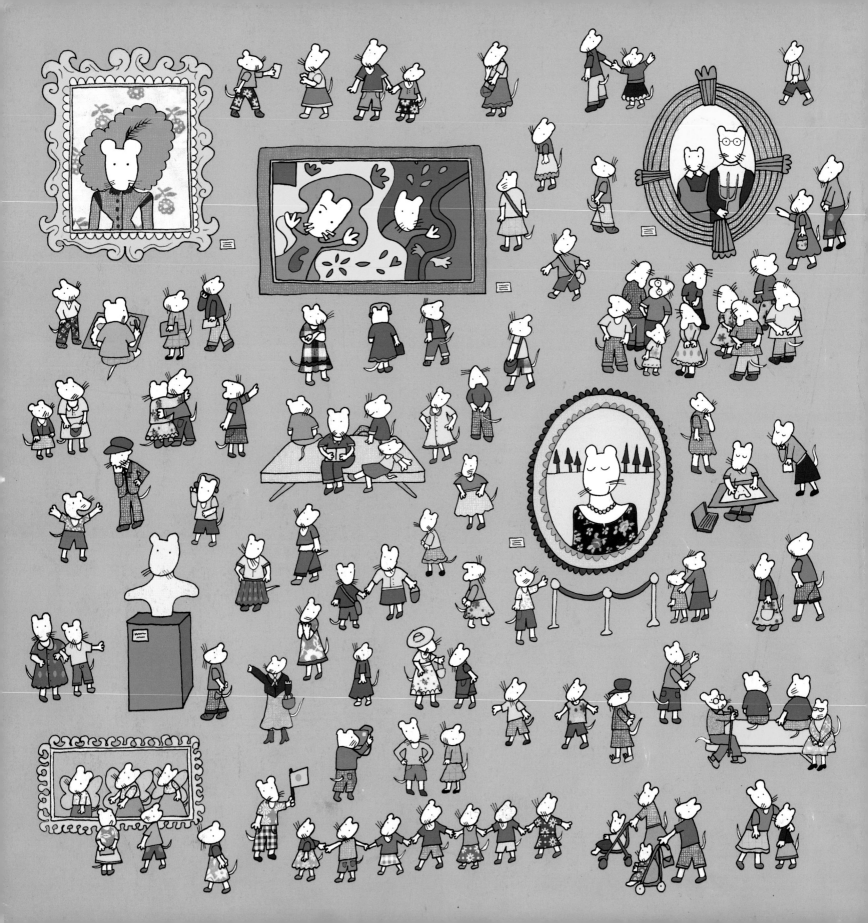

Mimi loves the gallery.
There's so much lovely art to see.

Can you spot **Mimi** drawing a **picture?**

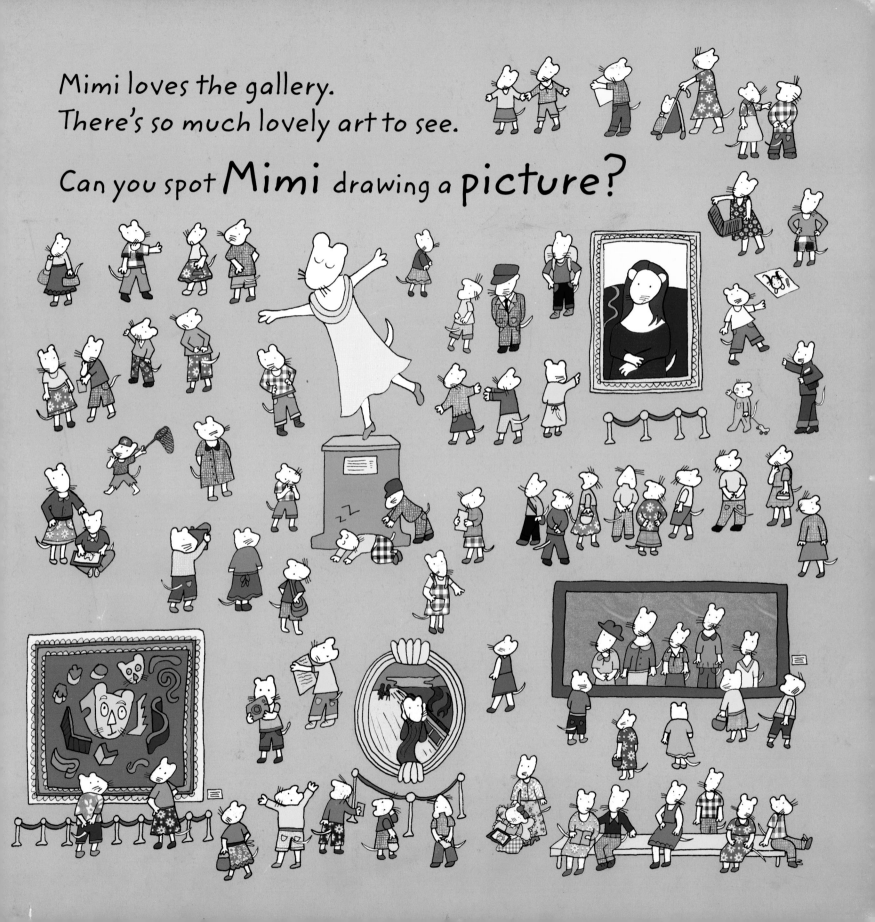

In the market, Mimi tries
Shoes and hats in every size!

Can you find Mimi and Molly trying on hats?

Mimi cycles down the track
Just behind her brother Mac.

Can you see Mimi and Mac cycling?

Look! Mimi's at the big fairground.
The ferris wheel takes her round and round.

Can you see Mimi and Grandma
on the big wheel?

MEETING POINT

strong mouse

5 4 3 2 1

BALL IN THE HOLE

candy
floss

It's karaoke — what a treat!

Mimi boogies to the beat.

Can you see Mimi dancing with Dad?

It's teatime at the big campsite
Then Mimi yawns and says goodnight!

Can you see **Mimi** in her **sleeping bag?**

MARKET
MUSEUM
Airport
WOODS
BEACH
TOWN

Start

11 Whoops, down the slide. Go back to 3.

10

12

13

14 Take a ride in the car straight to 27.

BUS STOP

3

2

1

4

5

9

15

16

6

7

8 You are having so much fun. Swim to 9.

17